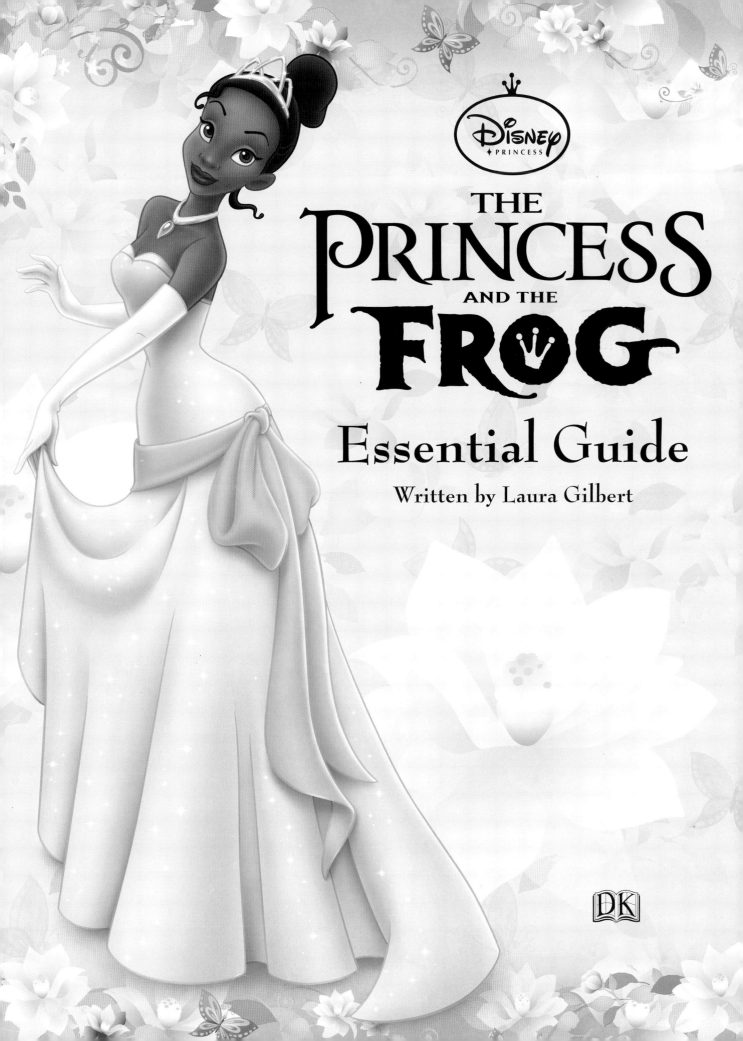

THE PRINCESS AND THE FROG

Essential Guide

Written by Laura Gilbert

Contents

Once Upon a Time   4–5
Tiana   6–7
Tiana's Family   8–9
Charlotte   10–11
Eli LaBouff   12–13
Duke's Diner   14–15
Tiana's Table   16–17
Naveen   18–19
Lawrence   20–21
Dr. Facilier   22–23
Masquerade Ball   24–25
The Bayou   26–27

Louis   28–29
Ray   30–31
Gone Frogging   32–33
Mama Odie   34–35
Frogs in Love   36–37
Down the River   38–39
Mardi Gras Wedding   40–41
Out of the Shadows   42–43
Happy Couple   44–45
Tiana's Palace   46–47
Acknowledgments   48

K ISSED THE FROG!

Then lo and behold, the frog was transformed into...

Once Upon a Time

Quite a few years ago, in a land not so far away, lived a young girl called Tiana. More than anything in the world she wanted to have her own restaurant where people could come to share delicious food and good company. However, with the help of a prince, an alligator, a firefly, and a bit of magic, Tiana would soon find out that what you want is not the same as what you need....

Tiana

Lots of girls want to be princesses when they grow up, but Tiana is different. She loves cooking and is determined to own a restaurant. The days fly by for Tiana as she works toward her goal but she doesn't mind: Every day that passes is a day closer to her dream.

"I don't have time for dancing!"

Princess Pals

Tiana has been best friends with Charlotte LaBouff since they were little girls. They used to love playing dress-up together.

Daddy's Girl

Tiana loves her father, James, very much. They often talk about their big plans. It's great to have someone to share your dreams with.

A sparkly crown is perfect for dressing up.

Tiana looks as pretty as a princess.

These long white gloves are an ideal accessory.

Go-getter

Tiana is ambitious. She has set her heart on turning an old sugar mill into a restaurant and will do whatever it takes to buy it.

Hard Worker

Tiana works as a waitress and doesn't have time to go to dances and balls like her best friend, Charlotte, does. But Tiana knows that one day, all her hard work will be worth it.

Tiana's Place

Tiana wants her restaurant to be the best in New Orleans. She is determined to make her family and friends very proud.

FACT FILE

Interests: Cooking
Ambition: Owning her own restaurant
Believes in: Working hard to fulfill her dreams

Tiana's mother, Eudora, made this beautiful blue dress for Charlotte.

Tiana's Family

Young Tiana lives with her mother, Eudora, and father, James, in New Orleans. Eudora is the best seamstress in town while James is an amazing cook. The pair teaches Tiana that you can have big dreams, but the only way you'll really succeed is through hard work.

Home, Sweet Home

The home where Eudora, James, and Tiana live is situated in the Ninth Ward of New Orleans. The family's house may be small but it is warm and welcoming and the door is always open to their friends and neighbors.

Good Times

Tiana's porch is often filled with people talking, singing, and eating delicious gumbo. Tiana's father was right: Good food puts smiles on people's faces.

What's Cooking?

When Tiana was little, James taught her how to cook. Father and daughter won many cooking contests and dreamed of starting their own restaurant.

Super seamstress Eudora makes dresses for Tiana's friend Charlotte. While Eudora sews, she often reads Tiana and Charlotte fairy-tale stories about princesses.

Loving Mother

Now Tiana is older, Eudora worries that she works too hard and that she will miss out on the important things, like love. Eudora wants nothing more for Tiana than for her to be happy, as Eudora was with James before he passed away.

Charlotte

Charlotte LaBouff lives with her rich daddy in a huge mansion. Ever since she was four years old, Charlotte has dreamed of being a princess. She's determined to do whatever it takes to get her prince, from wishing on the Evening Star to kissing a frog! Charlotte truly believes that one day her prince will come.

Princess's Parlor

Charlotte loves everything to do with princesses! Her room is filled with princess dolls, fairy-tale books about princesses, and a bed fit for a princess.

Sugar and Spice

Charlotte knows just how to wrap her father round her little finger. Big Daddy gives his sugarplum whatever she wants, whether it's a new dress or a new kitten.

"I would kiss a hundred frogs if I could marry a prince and be a princess!"

Sealed with a Kiss

Charlotte's favorite fairy tale says that the heroine has to kiss a frog to get her prince. Luckily, she's got her cat Marcel to practice on!

FACT FILE

Interests: Princess things
Ambition: To find her charming prince and become a princess
Believes in: Wishing

For daywear, Charlotte prefers a cloche hat to a tiara.

Charlotte has dozens of dresses, but her favorite ones are always pink!

Friends Indeed

Charlotte and Tiana are best friends. Charlotte knows that Tiana supports her princess dreams and hopes she can help her friend's dreams come true.

Pretty in Pink

Thanks to skilled seamstress Eudora, Charlotte's wardrobe is filled with hundreds of beautiful dresses for every occasion. For Mardi Gras or masquerade balls, Charlotte adds a tiara and a handful of sparkly glitter.

DID YOU KNOW?

Charlotte's favorite fairy tale is The Frog Prince. *After all, green goes perfectly with pink!*

Eli LaBouff

Eli LaBouff is the richest man in Louisiana. He made his vast fortune in sugar but the sweetest thing in his life is his daughter, Charlotte. Big Daddy may be tough in his business dealings, but he is really just a big guy with a very big heart.

The LaBouff Estate

The huge LaBouff mansion is situated on St. Charles Avenue in New Orleans. Beautiful flowers trail along the balcony and lacy curtains hang in the windows of the grand rooms. It looks like a fairy-tale castle, fit for a princess!

Big Softy

Eli only wants the best for his daughter, but his daughter wants a lot! He tries to be firm with her, but she always wins him over.

Despite being voted Mardi Gras King for five years in a row, Big Daddy still enjoys the honor!

"No more Mr. Pushover....
Now who wants a puppy?"

The High Life

Big Daddy is used to quality in all things. Eudora, the best seamstress in town, makes Charlotte's dresses and Eli eats at Duke's Diner, home of the greatest beignets in town. Only the best will do for Eli and his family!

Eli is a cheerful man who loves his life.

Like his daughter, Eli has all his clothes handmade.

FACT FILE

Interests: Beignets, Charlotte's happiness
Ambition: To keep Charlotte happy
Believes in: Charlotte's welfare...and beignets!

Duke's Diner

Whether you want the best beignets or delicious hotcakes, Duke's Diner is the place to be. Waitress Tiana knows she has to work hard to be able to have a restaurant of her own so she does a night shift at Cal's and a day shift at Duke's.

Violet wants Tiana to come out dancing.

Georgia worries that Tiana works too hard.

Sammy doesn't know how Tiana manages to work two jobs.

14

Cooking Up a Storm

Everyone eats at Duke's Diner, from Tiana's friends to the richest man in Louisiana, Eli LaBouff. Good food brings people together!

Customers love drinking a strong cup o' joe at Duke's Diner.

Tiana tries to remember that one day she'll have her own restaurant.

Some days tired Tiana can only tell which restaurant she's at by the color of her uniform!

Duke's Diner serves a variety of main meals.

Order Up!

Buford is the short order cook at Duke's. Happy to stay at the diner, he thinks Tiana's restaurant dreams are just that—dreams.

Tiana's Table

*F*ood has always been a huge part of Tiana's life, from cooking up bowls of delicious gumbo with her father to taking orders at Duke's Diner. Tiana knows that she'll be able to use everything she has learned when she opens her own restaurant. Tiana's Place will be the best in town!

Setting the Table

It is important that restaurant customers have everything they need to enjoy their meals, whether it's sharp knives to cut their steaks or spoons to stir their coffees.

Cutlery, Glassware, and Crockery

Cutlery	Drinking glass	Coffee cup	Bowl

Table 4
Food
3 beignets
1 flapjack

Drinks
2 coffees, 1 with milk, 1 without
1 orange juice

Tall Order

Tiana uses her notepad to take food and drink orders. With lots of people to serve, Tiana makes sure she clearly writes down table numbers and customers' exact requirements.

Service with a Smile

Being a waitress means you have to be able to do lots of things at once! While Tiana is serving customers food at one table, another diner may be wanting to place an order.

MENU

Mains and Desserts

Sausages, eggs, and fries
Have your eggs any way you like: Sunny side up, over easy, or scrambled. Our chef can do them all!

Gumbo
Our most popular dish. This gumbo has a special ingredient to make it different from any other—a few drops of hot sauce.

Fresh fruit platter
Whether it's juicy oranges or sweet grapes, our fruit platters are always a hit with the customers. Also goes well with grits.

Snacks

Grits
Delicious any time of the day. Can be served with cheese, vegetables, or just as it comes!

Beignets
Our beignets are the best in town! Perfect as a breakfast snack or just for a treat.

Drinks

Soda
A refreshing soda served in a glass with ice and lemon. Goes well with our famous gumbo.

Orange juice
Freshly squeezed orange juice is healthy *and* delicious!

Coffee
The perfect start to the day! Why not try a cup with one of our delicious beignets?

Dining Dreams

While she works at Duke's Diner, Tiana dreams of the day when she will have her own restaurant. At Tiana's Place, she'll cook her beignets, but there will be plenty of other delicious dishes on the menu.

Naveen

Behold—Prince Naveen of Maldonia! This royal has come to New Orleans to experience the birthplace of his greatest love—jazz. Handsome Naveen (his words!) is easily distracted by pretty women and music, but one day this spoiled prince will have to grow up.

Naughty Naveen

Naveen has been cut out of his inheritance by his parents, the king and queen of Maldonia. They are disappointed that Naveen prefers parties to royal responsibilities.

"All women enjoy the kiss of Prince Naveen."

Prince Charming

Naveen is certainly popular with the ladies! In Naveen's eyes, all women are princesses. He loves to serenade his admirers, plucking at their heart strings.

MALDONIAN MOTTOES

Abinaza: See you later
Achidanza: Cool!
Faldi faldonza: Oh my word!
De Fragee Pruto: The Frog Prince

Naveen never has a hair out of place.

Proud Naveen wears anything that makes him look good.

Music to his Ears

Naveen adores jazz and dancing. When he hears those horns playing, he just can't keep his feet still.

Pampered Prince

Born into royalty, Prince Naveen has never had to lift a finger. He had servants to dress him, to feed him, and to brush his teeth. Now that Naveen's parents have disowned him, he realizes he doesn't know how to do anything for himself!

FACT FILE

Interests: Princesses, jazz
Ambition: To be rich
Believes in: Having riches without having to work for them

When Naveen's valet, Lawrence, tries to keep the prince on schedule, Naveen doesn't listen. He thinks Lawrence should just relax!

Lawrence

Prince Naveen's valet is the portly Lawrence. Poor Lawrence has been pushed around all his life, first by his family and now by Naveen. But he is very good at his job and Naveen would be completely lost without him—literally! Lawrence just wishes Prince Naveen appreciated him a little more.

Daily Duties

Lawrence's day is spent making sure Prince Naveen arrives on time, has all the right clothes, and doesn't get distracted. Lawrence spends so much time thinking about the prince that he has no time to think about himself.

Prince's Protector

Naveen pushes his valet around, but he should listen to him. When sinister Dr. Facilier tells Naveen he knows he is a prince, Naveen thinks it's magic, but Lawrence knows Facilier has read the news of Naveen's arrival!

Dear Diary,
Another awful day spent looking after his highness. Today he even made me dance— oh, the humiliation! One day, I'll get my own back....

Big Dreams

Lawrence's greatest wish is to be a prince. Everyone respects royalty, all the women love a prince, and Lawrence could have his very own valet! Well, a man can dream....

Green with Envy

While he would never admit it, Lawrence is jealous of Naveen. He wishes he were as handsome and charming as the prince. Naveen is respected by everyone and Lawrence wishes he were, too.

Lawrence is always cleanly shaved because he is always working!

A valet must always be formally dressed.

"I just need a moment to compose myself!"

Lawrence is very light on his feet when he dances.

FACT FILE

Interests: Royalty

Ambition: To be the man he has always wanted to be

Believes in: Respect for others and for himself

Dr. Facilier

Those who enter Dr. Facilier's emporium—beware! With the shadows by his side, this doctor of bad magic claims to be able to make dreams come true, but really he turns them into nightmares. Dr. Facilier has his eye on the LaBouff fortune and is determined to use his magic to become wealthy.

Tricky Business

Dr. Facilier knows all the tricks in the book, from fortune-telling to preparing magical potions. However, he can't use magic on himself. So when a rich prince and his valet turn up on his doorstep, Dr. Facilier sees a magical opportunity.

Sinister Shop

Dr. Facilier's emporium is packed with strange and magical things, such as decorated skulls, jars filled with unusual powders, and weird-looking dolls.

Summoning Shadows

Even though he has his own magic shadow, Dr. Facilier needs some more help. So, he calls on shadows from the other side to assist him in his search for riches. These powerful dark visions can make anyone do exactly what they—and Facilier—want them to.

Into the Future

Dr. Facilier can read people's futures. When he reads Naveen and Lawrence's cards, Facilier sees riches for the prince and a crown for the valet—provided they shake on it first....

When he needs extra help, Facilier summons more sinister shadows.

Facilier's shadow always stays with him.

A walking cane is useful for keeping those shadows at bay.

"...charms, potions, dreams made real."

Charming Charmer

Bewitching Dr. Facilier can lure anyone into thinking he can give them what they desire. The truth is, he usually leaves them worse off than they were! This evil magician is really only interested in looking after number one.

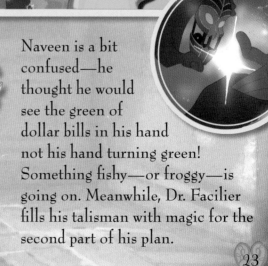

FACT FILE

Interests: Money
Ambition: Getting his hands on the LaBouff family fortune
Believes in: Bad magic

Naveen is a bit confused—he thought he would see the green of dollar bills in his hand not his hand turning green! Something fishy—or froggy—is going on. Meanwhile, Dr. Facilier fills his talisman with magic for the second part of his plan.

Masquerade Ball

Eli LaBouff loves to throw lavish parties at his estate. This year's masquerade ball is extra special—Prince Naveen of Maldonia is attending. The prince is the perfect guest. After all, he won't need to find a costume, and Eli's precious Charlotte thinks his highness is simply the bee's knees!

Charlotte says she never gets anything she wishes for, but now Prince Naveen is coming to the ball—or so she thinks....

Fancy Dress

The people dressed as sheep, witches, and saxophones aren't the only ones in disguise. Thanks to Dr. Facilier's magic talisman, Lawrence looks like Prince Naveen. All Facilier needs is for Lawrence to marry Charlotte and the LaBouff fortune will be in his sights.

Party Palace

Colored lanterns lead Louisiana's elite up the steps of the LaBouff mansion for the masquerade ball. While the orchestra plays, medieval waiters and waitresses serve food to the many guests.

Tiana can't wait to sign the papers for the sugar mill. But the greedy estate brokers tell her unless she pays more, her restaurant dreams are over. These two aren't horsing around!

Fairy-Tale Kiss

When Tiana's dress is ruined, she borrows one of Charlotte's. Then a frog calling himself Prince Naveen says he can give Tiana all the money she needs if she will kiss him and turn him back into a human. This is the weirdest fairy tale Tiana's ever heard!

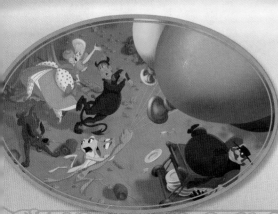

One kiss later and Tiana is hopping mad to find that, like Naveen, she is a frog. The scared duo grab some balloons so they can get out of there!

The Bayou

The muddy and swampy bayou is home to all sorts of weird and wonderful creatures, such as alligators, fireflies, and even snakes. Most visitors arrive by boat, but Tiana and Naveen have drifted here by balloon. This froggy pair should be at home on land and in water, but they're struggling to find their sea legs.

Spooky Trees

At first glance, the trees that tower over the bayou are a bit creepy. If you look very carefully you might see an old boat in one. But twigs from the trees come in useful if you need to make a raft or...a jazz ukelele.

Fast Food

It's not just the creatures in the water that you have to worry about—there are plenty in the air. Naveen just wants these pesky mosquitoes and flies to buzz off, but then he realizes that they make quite a tasty snack if you're a frog!

Looking for a Bite

Logs float down the bayou, but look closely and you'll see that some of them have eyes and very sharp teeth! Tiana and Naveen take shelter in a tree while the gators snap at their heels.

Naveen thinks the bayou is the scariest place he's ever visited.

Flying Fish

The closest Tiana has got to fish is when she cooks one. In the bayou, they are absolutely everywhere! The waters are filled with shrimp, crawfish, and huge leaping catfish.

Sticking Point

What's small, slimy, and won't leave Naveen alone? No, it's not Tiana—it's a leech! Naveen doesn't know what to do when one lands on his arm, but Tiana comes to the rescue—as usual!

DID YOU KNOW?

The word "bayou" means "small stream." Now, that doesn't sound at all scary, does it?

Louis

Louis is one jazz-loving alligator. His dream is to play his trumpet in a real-life jazz band, but he thinks he'll only be able to do that if he magically becomes human! This green gator never snaps at anyone and truly has a heart of gold.

Bayou Blues

Laid-back Louis taught himself to play the trumpet by listening to people playing jazz on the bayou riverboats. Those guys are the best in the business and Louis hopes to be, too.

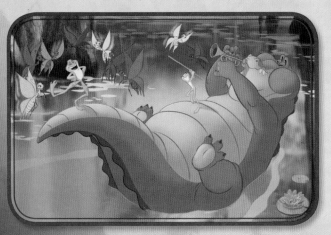

Helping Hand

When Louis gets covered in sharp thorns from a prickly pricker bush, his firefly friend Ray is on hand to help him out.

Gator Gumbo

Louis's taste buds go dancing when he thinks about food. His dream meal would be crawfish smothered in remoulade sauce followed by Bananas Foster sprinkled with pralines.

Stand clear when this tail's a' swiping!

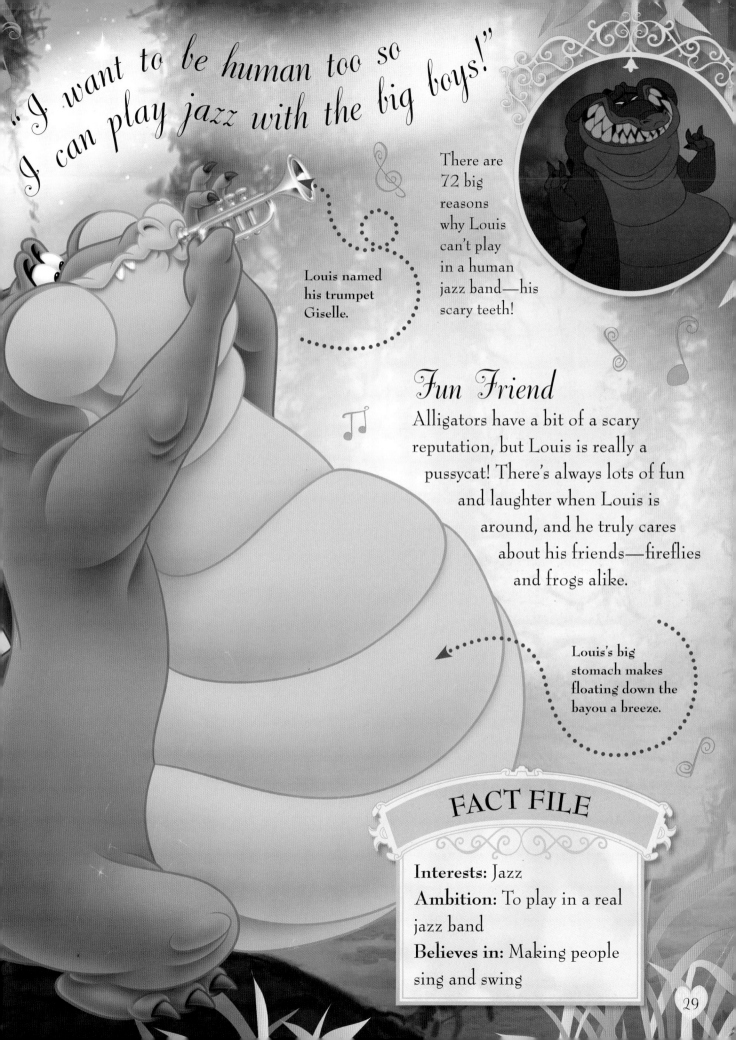

" I want to be human too so I can play jazz with the big boys!"

Louis named his trumpet Giselle.

There are 72 big reasons why Louis can't play in a human jazz band—his scary teeth!

Fun Friend

Alligators have a bit of a scary reputation, but Louis is really a pussycat! There's always lots of fun and laughter when Louis is around, and he truly cares about his friends—fireflies and frogs alike.

Louis's big stomach makes floating down the bayou a breeze.

FACT FILE

Interests: Jazz
Ambition: To play in a real jazz band
Believes in: Making people sing and swing

Ray

Born and bred in the bayou, firefly Ray is a true Cajun. Laid-back and easygoing, he always looks on the bright side of life. Ray absolutely adores his friends and believes that all you need in life is love. This upbeat little firefly is a true ray of light!

See the Light

Ray knows there is always a way out of a tricky situation. Whether it's untangling two tongue-tied frogs, pulling thorns from Louis's skin, or flying up the nose of a froghunter, Ray saves the day!

Party On!
Ray loves a good soiree. He's got his own lighting system, and with Lulu the caterpillar making the music, the party can get started!

Ray's Family
Ray has a big firefly family, including Mimi, Henri, Celeste, Grandma, Randy, Pookie, and Angela. Ray's "relationals" are always buzzing around the bayou.

"Let me shine a little light on the situation..."

Evangeline shines brightly in the night sky.

Lights Out

Even a firefly can have an off day! Ray sometimes has trouble lighting up, but his power of positive thought always wins through.

Love at First Light

Ray is head over wings in love with Evangeline. He talks to her every night but she is one shy firefly—or so Ray thinks. What Ray doesn't know is Evangeline is actually the Evening Star! Will this starstruck pair ever be together?

Ray is a hopeless romantic and he loves Evangeline.

Ray's wings help him navigate through the bayou.

FACT FILE

Interests: Evangeline, the light of his life
Ambition: To be with Evangeline
Believes in: True love

Ray can write his name in the sky using his light.

Gone Frogging

If froghunter Reggie and his sons, Darnell and Two Fingers, had to rely on their wits, they'd never catch anything! Luckily for them, Naveen and Tiana are distracted in the bayou, and it only takes a moment for Reggie to net Naveen and for Darnell to catch Tian[a]

Darnell can't believe it when Tiana talks to him!

Two Fingers is just as dopey as his brother.

Tiana is determined not to stay in this cage for long.

Frog Freedom

The froghunters try to stop their prisoners from escaping, but the silly trio miss their targets. They only manage to do damage to themselves, while Tiana and Naveen flee. It looks like Reggie and the boys will go home empty-handed.

Dinner Time

Reggie and his growing boys can't wait to have their dinner tonight. How do frogs' legs with cornbread and sauce picant sound? Naveen and Tiana certainly don't like the sound of it!

A bug's got to do what a bug's got to do, so Ray flies up Reggie's nose to free Naveen.

Naveen is not sure how he's going to get out of this mess.

Mama Odie

Mama Odie is the queen of good magic. This 197-year-old blind lady lives with her snake, Juju, in a shrimp boat wedged in a tree. There she makes magical gumbo that conjures up visions of the future. Naveen and Tiana only hope Mama Odie can help them.

Words of Wisdom

Tiana and Naveen want Mama Odie to make them human. But wise Mama Odie explains that what you *need* and what you *want* are two different things. To be happy they must find out what they truly need.

"Gumbo, gumbo in the pot—we need a princess, what you got?"

Mama Odie tells Naveen and Tiana that if they want to be human and fulfill their dreams, Naveen must kiss a princess before midnight. As Mama Odie looks in her gumbo, Charlotte appears. She may be a Mardi Gras princess but she'll do!

To get to Mama Odie's house, you must avoid the pricker bushes, traps, and, worst of all, the hunters!

Snake Eyes

Mama Odie loves her trusty milk snake, Juju. Whether it's adding hot sauce to the gumbo, transforming himself into a walking cane, or keeping Mama Odie's neck warm, Juju is always around to help. This snake's a real charmer!

Mama Odie may be blind, but she knows these steps like the back of her hand.

Mama Odie may be little but she has a big heart.

FACT FILE

Interests: Good magic
Ambition: Mama Odie has all she needs
Believes in: Knowing who you are and what you need

Frogs in Love

Tiana and Naveen are as different a
can be. Tiana works hard, serving
platters of food at Duke's, while Navee
has had everything handed to him on a
silver platter. But the
more time they spend
together, the more they
seem to get along.

Tiana to the Rescue!

Tiana knows how to look out for herself. It is
Tiana who swats the butterflies out of the way, while
Naveen just tries to sweet-talk them. She wonders
if Naveen will ever learn to pull his weight.

Naveen takes it easy
as Tiana steers the
twig raft along the
bayou. Tiana is
not surprised at
lazy Naveen!

Music-lover
Naveen made
his own ukelele.

Food of Love

Naveen thinks he can sit around waiting for Tiana to cook, but Tiana has other ideas. She is determined to get this spoiled frog working, so she shows him how to mince some yummy mushrooms.

"Tiana...she is my Evangeline."

Dance Partners

Tiana has never danced so Naveen teaches her. If Naveen can learn how to cut up vegetables, Tiana can learn how to cut a rug!

Tiana is surprised to find herself falling for Naveen.

True Love

Naveen realizes he loves Tiana, warts and all. He tells Ray all about it but he is yet to tell Tiana. It's lucky that little Ray has a big mouth!

All Change

At the start, Naveen was annoyed because he thought Tiana was a princess and Tiana was angry at Naveen when she turned into a frog. But Tiana makes Naveen laugh and she realizes that she likes Naveen!

Down the River

There is no better way to travel down the Mississippi than by steamboat. This boat is filled with people in Mardi Gras costume enjoying the Dixieland music, the Cajun food, and the beautiful views. Tiana, Naveen, Louis, and Ray see the chance to hitch a ride to the Mardi Gras parade, so they hop aboard.

Romantic Cruise

Naveen isn't able to tell Tiana he loves her—she is too distracted by thoughts of her restaurant. Naveen decides that if kissing Charlotte is what it takes to help Tiana fulfill her dream then that's what he'll do.

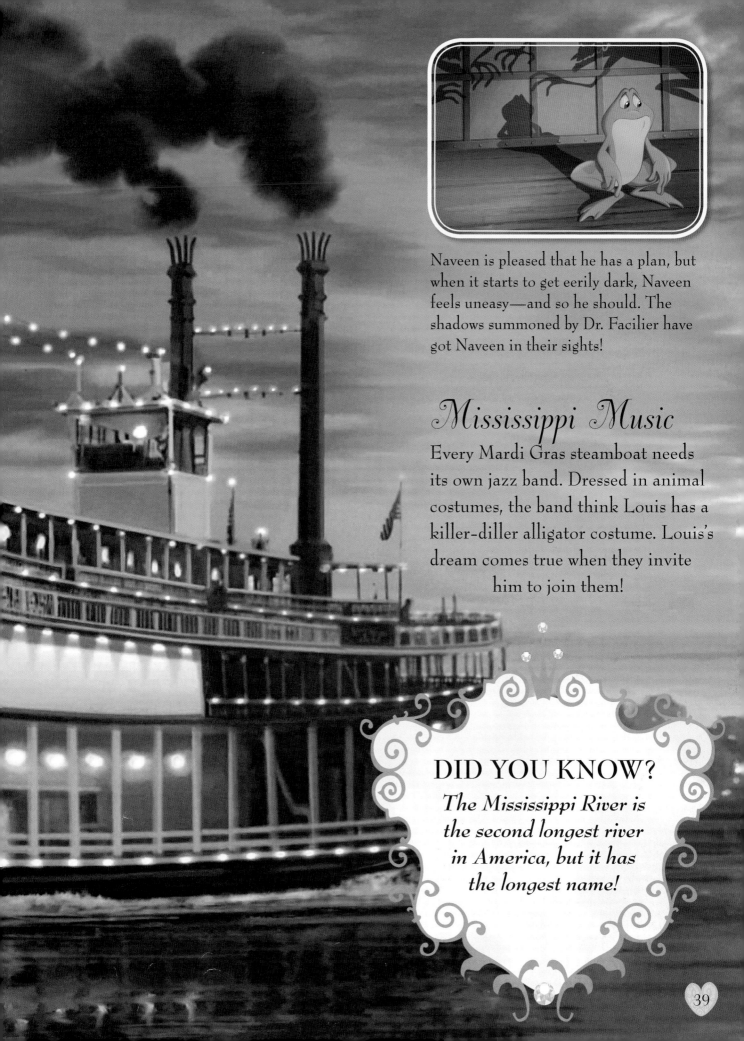

Naveen is pleased that he has a plan, but when it starts to get eerily dark, Naveen feels uneasy—and so he should. The shadows summoned by Dr. Facilier have got Naveen in their sights!

Mississippi Music

Every Mardi Gras steamboat needs its own jazz band. Dressed in animal costumes, the band think Louis has a killer-diller alligator costume. Louis's dream comes true when they invite him to join them!

DID YOU KNOW?

The Mississippi River is the second longest river in America, but it has the longest name!

Mardi Gras Wedding

It's carnival time! In New Orleans, everyone takes to the streets to enjoy the party atmosphere of Mardi Gras. This year's Mardi Gras is special. Charlotte will become a true princess when she marries Prince Naveen—or so she thinks. Unfortunately for Charlotte, being Mardi Gras princess may be the closest she will get to royalty.

This horse is much bigger than the real ones pulling the floats!

There's always lots of royalty at Mardi Gras.

Dream Come True

When Lawrence, as Naveen, proposes to Charlotte, all Charlotte can think about is the dress and the flowers. All Lawrence can think about is making sure that Charlotte doesn't realize who he truly is.

The band drums up cheers from the crowd.

Carnival Costumes

Everyone gets into the carnival spirit at Mardi Gras and dresses up in costume. The elaborate floats carry people dressed as genies, mermaids, and pirates.

The happy couple stand on top of a giant wedding cake as Reverend Tolliver begins the wedding ceremony. Charlotte's proud father looks on.

Colorful jesters on stilts march alongside giant chefs.

Last Chance

Having escaped from the grasp of Dr. Facilier and his shadows, Naveen knows that he must kiss Charlotte before she marries Lawrence. Naveen makes a grab for Lawrence's talisman in order to turn Lawrence back to his true self.

Out of the Shadows

Dr. Facilier is just moments away from fulfilling his plan, if only the annoying wildlife would get out of the way! Tiana, Naveen, Ray, and Louis are not what the doctor needs right now. Will evil Facilier's bad magic put an end to Tiana's and Naveen's dreams forever?

Fleeing Firefly

As Naveen tries to grab the magic talisman, Lawrence grabs Naveen. However, Naveen manages to snatch the charm using his tongue, and Lawrence turns back into his portly self. Realizing he is in a tricky situation, Naveen tosses the talisman to Ray for safekeeping.

Last Chance

Ray quickly passes the talisman to Tiana. Poor Ray is just in time, as the shadows close in on him and Facilier swats him away. The doctor sees the last chance for his plan to work, and blows a magic cloud over Tiana to reveal her future.

Shattered Dreams

Tiana's restaurant only exists in her imagination. Dr. Facilier can make it real—if she hands over the talisman. Tiana realizes the restaurant may be what she *wants*, but what she *needs* are Naveen and her friends and family, so she smashes the talisman.

Evil End

While Lawrence is arrested, Dr. Facilier faces a darker doom. With the talisman destroyed, the sinister shadows turn on Dr. Facilier.

Friend in Need

Naveen says he will marry Charlotte to make Tiana's dream a reality, but Tiana doesn't want to lose Naveen. Charlotte agrees to kiss Naveen to make the pair's dreams come true.

Lucky Star

Ray managed to help his pals before the shadows and Dr. Facilier caught up with him. Ray's friends can't believe he is gone, but then they see a new star in the sky. Ray's firefly light may have been dimmed forever, but at least he and Evangeline are finally together.

Happy Couple

Charlotte has read lots of fairy tales about romance and knows that Tiana and Naveen are truly in love. Just as the clock chimes midnight, Charlotte kisses Naveen to break the spell, but she is too late—Tiana and Naveen are still frogs.

Devoted Duo

Naveen and Tiana may not have turned back into humans, but at least they have each other. Many people would be green with envy looking at this loving couple.

"My dream wouldn't be complete...without you in it."

Perfect Partners

Mama Odie pronounces Naveen and Tiana frog and wife. As the pair kiss, magic dust swirls around them and they become human. By marrying Naveen, Tiana has become a princess, and by kissing a princess, the spell has been broken!

Happily Ever After

After their froggy wedding, Tiana and Naveen hop along to the church to have a human one! Their family and friends join the celebration, and Charlotte catches Tiana's bouquet. Maybe Charlotte's princess dream will come true....

Tiana's Palace

Tiana can't believe it! With a little bit of wishing and a lot of hard work, Tiana has the restaurant she always wanted. Even better than that, she has made new friends she will never forget. It's a fairy tale come true!

Frogs will always have a special place in Tiana's heart.

Prince Naveen and his princess dance on the rooftop of Tiana's Palace as Ray and Evangeline sparkle in the sky above.

Crystal chandeliers light up the restaurant's rooms.

Sweet Dreams

The sugar mill needed a lot of work, but Tiana and Naveen were able to turn it into the restaurant of their dreams. Tiana knows that her father, James, would be very proud of Tiana's Palace.

Customers come from miles around to enjoy Tiana's delicious food.

Happy Ending

Tiana's father used to say: Good food brings people together. Tiana is glad she can share her restaurant with family and friends, and with Naveen by her side, Tiana finally has all she needs.

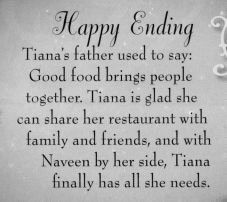

Every night, Tiana's Palace is alive with music and laughter.

DID YOU KNOW?

Young Tiana wanted to call her restaurant "Tiana's Place." Now that she's older, Tiana prefers "Tiana's Palace."

DK

LONDON, NEW YORK,
MELBOURNE, MUNICH, AND DELHI

Designer Julie Thompson
Senior Editor Laura Gilbert
Managing Editor Catherine Saunders
Art Director Lisa Lanzarini
Publishing Manager Simon Beecroft
Category Publisher Alex Allan
Production Editor Siu Yin Chan
Print Production Nick Seston

First published in the United States in 2009
by DK Publishing
375 Hudson Street
New York, New York 10014

09 10 11 12 13 10 9 8 7 6 5 4 3 2

175429 – 07/09

DK books are available at special discounts when purchased in bulk for sales
promotions, premiums, fundraising, or educational use. For details, contact:
DK Publishing Special Markets,
375 Hudson Street, New York, New York 10014
SpecialSales@dk.com

A catalog record for this book is
available from the Library of Congress.

ISBN: 978-0-7566-5542-6

Color reproduction by Alta Image, UK
Printed and bound by Lake Books, USA

Discover more at
www.dk.com